First published 1989 by Julia MacRae Books
This edition published 1997 by Walker Books Ltd
87 Vauxhall Walk, London SE11 5HJ

10 9 8 7 6

Printed in Hong Kong

British Library Cataloguing in Publication Data
A catalogue record for this book is available
from the British Library

ISBN 0-7445-5239-7

THE TUNNEL

ANTHONY BROWNE

WALKER BOOKS
AND SUBSIDIARIES
LONDON • BOSTON • SYDNEY

Once upon a time there lived a sister and brother who were not at all alike. In every way they were different.

The sister stayed inside on her own, reading and dreaming. The brother played outside with his friends, laughing and shouting, throwing and kicking, roughing and tumbling.

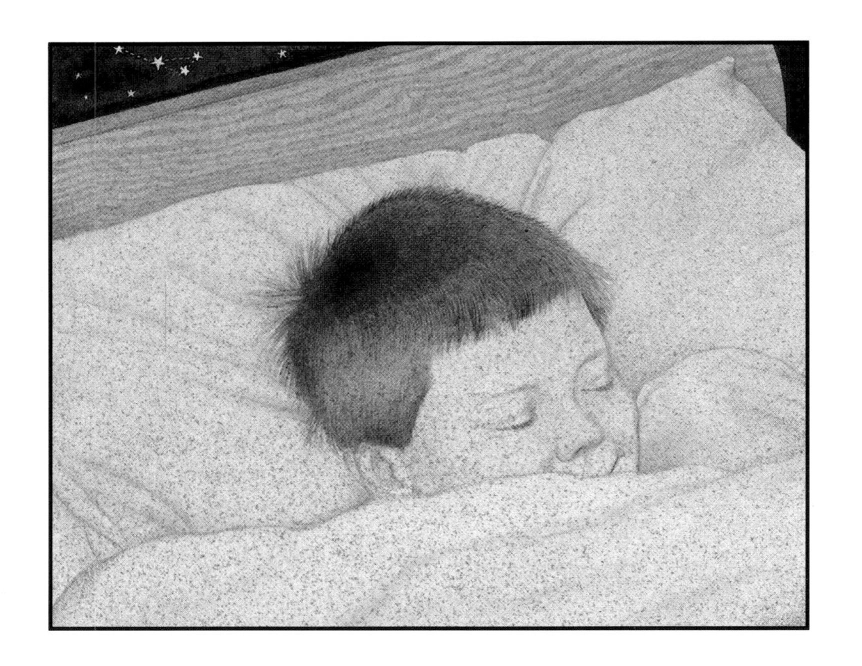

At night he slept soundly in his room. But she would lie awake, listening to the noises of the night. Sometimes he crept into her room to frighten her, for he knew that she was afraid of the dark.

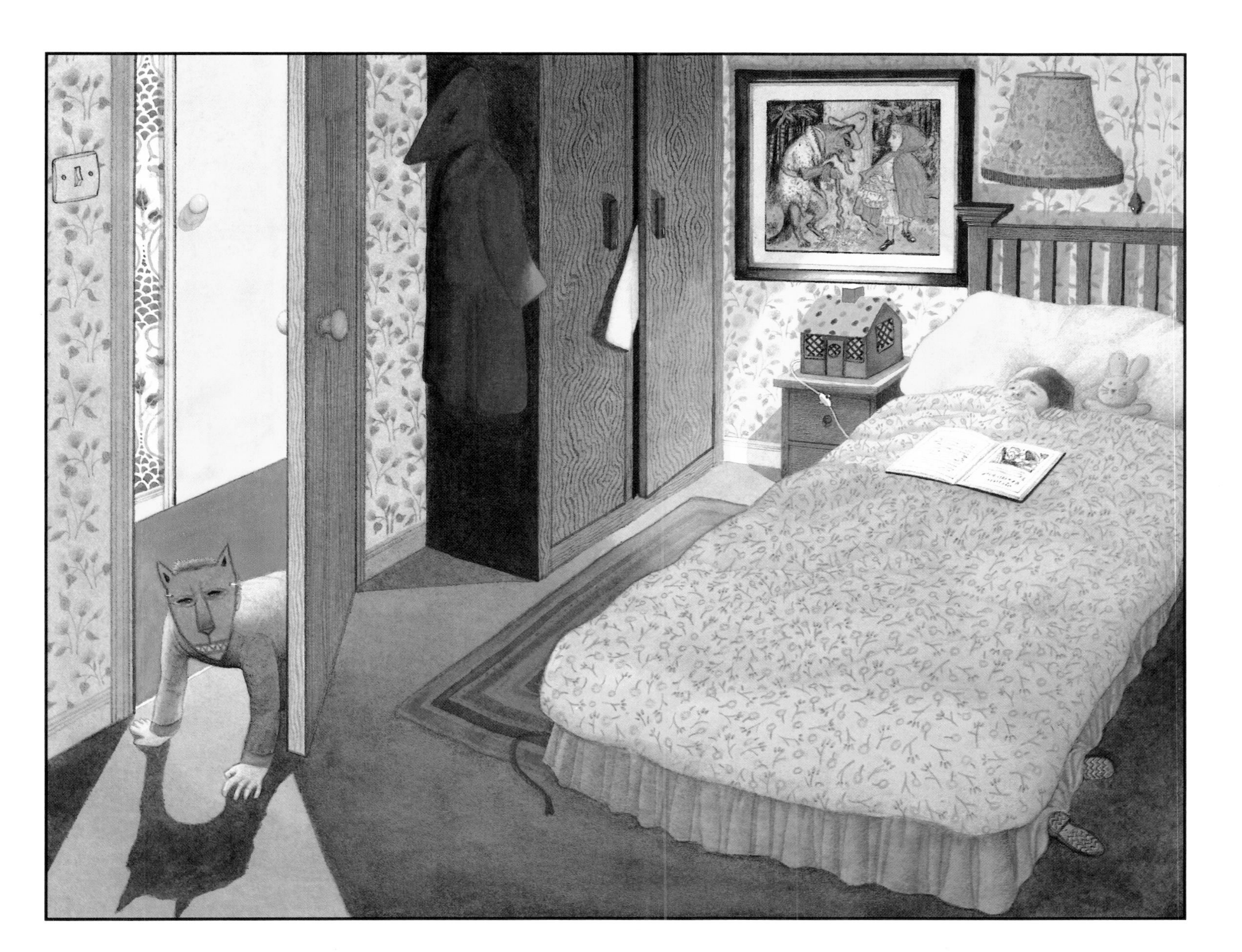

Whenever they were together they fought and argued noisily.
All the time.

One morning their mother grew impatient with them. "Out you go together," she said, "and try to be nice to each other just for once. And be back in time for lunch." But the boy didn't want his little sister with him.

They went to a piece of waste ground.
"Why did you have to come?" he moaned.
"It's not my fault," she said. "I didn't want to come to this awful place. It scares me."
"Oh, you baby," said her brother. "You're frightened of everything."
He went off to explore.

“**H**ey! Come here!” he yelled a little while later. She walked over to him.

“Look!” he said. “A tunnel! Come on, let’s see what’s at the other end.”

“N-no, you mustn’t,” she said. “There might be witches . . . or goblins . . . or *anything* down there.”

“Don’t be so wet,” said her brother. “That’s kid’s stuff.”

“We have to be back by lunchtime . . .” she said.

His sister was frightened of the tunnel and so she waited for him to come out again. She waited and waited, but he did not come. She was close to tears. What could she do? She *had* to follow him into the tunnel.

The tunnel was dark,

and damp, and slimy, and scary.

At the other end she found herself in a quiet wood. There was no sign of her brother. But the wood soon turned into a dark forest. She thought about wolves and giants and witches, and wanted to turn back, but she could not – for what would become of her brother if she did? By now she was very frightened and she began to run, faster and faster . . .

Just when she knew she could run no further,
she came to a clearing.
There was a figure, still as stone.
It was her brother.
"Oh no!" she sobbed. "I'm too late."

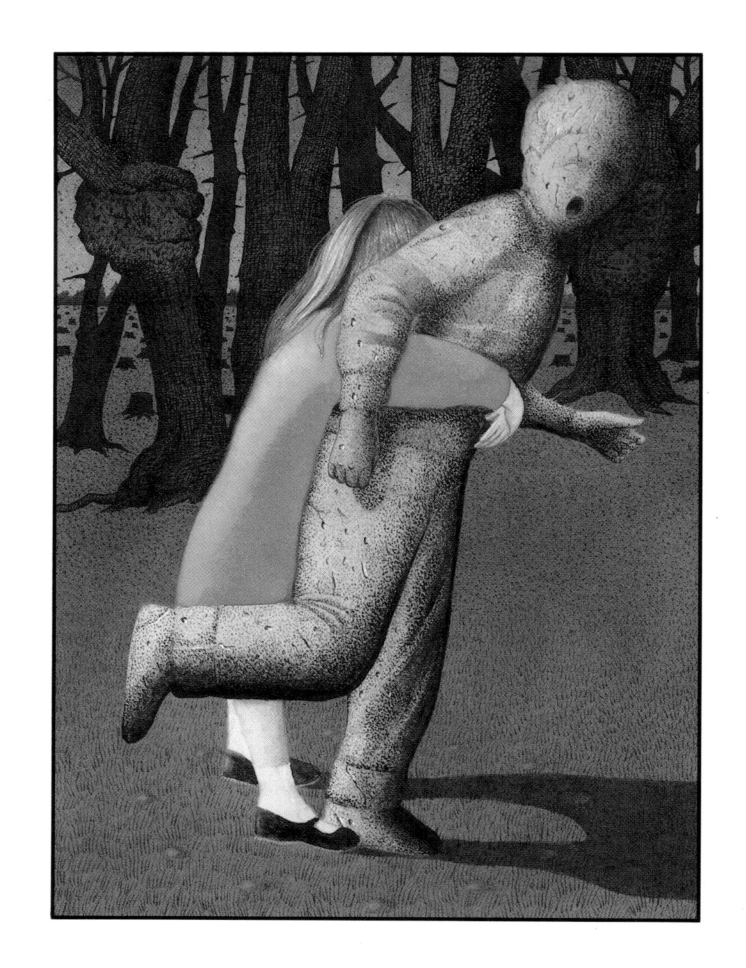

She threw her arms around the cold hard form, and wept. Very slowly, the figure began to change colour, becoming softer and warmer.

Then, little by little, it began to move. Her brother was there. “Rose! I knew you’d come,” he said. They ran back, through the forest, through the wood, into the tunnel, and out again. Together.

When they reached home, their mother was setting the table.
"Hello," she said, "you two seem very quiet.
Is everything all right?"
Rose smiled at her brother.
And Jack smiled back.

MORE WALKER PAPERBACKS

For You to Enjoy

Also by Anthony Browne

GORILLA

Winner of the Kate Greenaway Medal and Kurt Maschler Award,
this is the classic story of a lonely girl, a friendly gorilla and their amazing night out.

"Joyous and moving... A tour de force." *The Times Literary Supplement*

0-7445-9997-0 £4.99

Jeremy, it seems, has everything, but he won't share anything with Sam.
Could it be, though, that Sam has something far more valuable?

"A stunning visual experience for the sharp-eyed, this is also a book which has a message for the thoughtful reader." *Junior Education*

0-7445-4372-X £4.99

HANSEL AND GRETEL

"One of the most exciting new versions of a popular tale ever." *Parents*

"Strong, clean, clear pictures ... an unusual sensitivity to the emotional resonance of the story." *The Times Educational Supplement*

0-7445-4364-9 £4.99

Walker Paperbacks are available from most booksellers, or by post from B.B.C.S., P.O. Box 941, Hull, North Humberside HU1 3YQ
24 hour telephone credit card line 01482 224626

To order, send: Title, author, ISBN number and price for each book ordered, your full name and address, cheque or postal order payable to BBCS for the total amount and allow the following for postage and packing:
UK and BFPO: £1.00 for the first book, and 50p for each additional book to a maximum of £3.50.
Overseas and Eire: £2.00 for the first book, £1.00 for the second and 50p for each additional book.
Prices and availability are subject to change without notice.